To Brian, the worst liar I know. — cj

Little ✷ BOOST is published by
Picture Window Books, a Capstone Imprint
1710 Roe Crest Drive
North Mankato, Minnesota 56003
www.capstonepub.com

Library of Congress Cataloging-in-Publication Data
Jones, Christianne C.
Hello, goodbye, and a very little lie / by Christianne
Jones ; illustrated by Christine Battuz.
p. cm. — (Little boost)
ISBN 978-1-5158-1878-6 (saddle-stitch)
[1. Honesty—Fiction.] I. Battuz, Christine, ill. II. Title.
PZ7.J6823He 2011
[E]—dc22   2010004665

Summary: Larry lies about practically everything until
he meets a girl who outsmarts him.

Creative Direction: Heather Kindseth
Art Direction/Graphic Design: Kay Fraser

Printed in China.
005007

Hello Goodbye

and a very little lie

by Christianne Jones

illustrated by Christine Battuz

PICTURE WINDOW BOOKS

a capstone imprint

Larry is a liar.

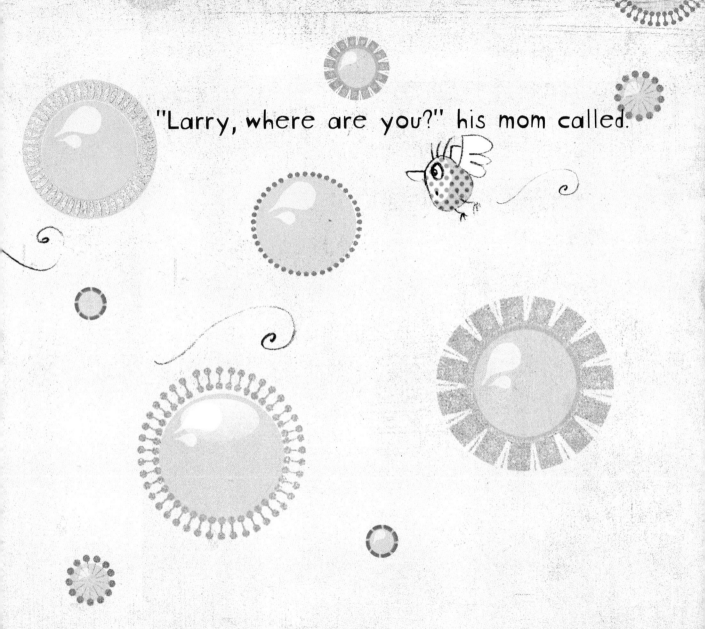

"Larry, where are you?" his mom called.

"I'm doing my homework," Larry lied.

"Larry, don't eat all the frosting," his mom said.

"I'm not," Larry lied.

"Larry, why do you lie so much?"

his mom asked.

"I'm not lying,"
Larry replied.

"Oh, Larry," his mom said with a sigh.

"No one is going to listen to you
if you keep lying," his dad said.

"Dad, people always listen to me," Larry said.

At the park, Larry talked while the others played.

Hello. I'm Larry. I built this playground. **GOODBYE.**

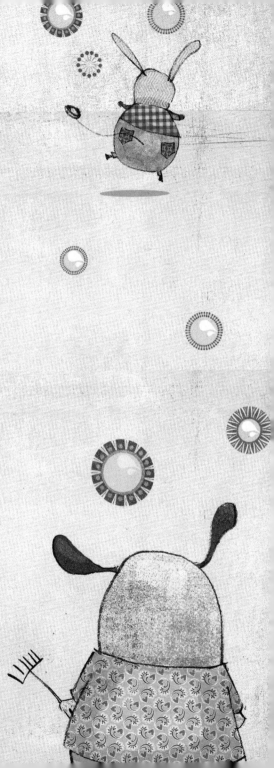

At the grocery store, Larry stopped
stranger after stranger.

At the library, Larry loudly exclaimed,

Hello. I'm Larry.
I have read every
one of these books.
GOODBYE.

One sunny Saturday, Larry was on his way
to the beach when he saw a spunky little
girl reading a magazine.

But before he could speed away, the girl

stopped him.

"No, you can't," she said.

"Yes, I CAN,"

Larry said.

Larry looked across to the other side
of the lake.

The lake was
REALLY, REALLY BIG.

"I don't see your ball," said Larry.

"It's really far away," said the girl.

Larry knew he couldn't swim all the way across the lake.

There was only one thing left for Larry to do.
He jumped into the water, turned to the small
crowd, and declared,

"**GOODBYE**," said the crowd. And they walked away.

"Wait!" Larry yelled.

"Do you think two liars could stop lying and be friends?" Larry asked.

"**No,**" said the girl.

Then she started to laugh. "That was a lie. Let's be friends."

And from that day on, Larry never, ever,
EVER told another lie again.

Or so we think.

To my dad, Amos. You get what you get . . .
and I'm so thankful I got you. -jg

 is published by
Picture Window Books, A Capstone Imprint
1710 Roe Crest Drive
North Mankato, Minnesota 56003
www.capstonepub.com

Library of Congress Cataloging-in-Publication data is
available on the Library of Congress website.

ISBN: 978-1-5158-1880-9 (saddle-stitch)

Designer: Hilary Wacholz

Printed and bound in China.
005007

YOU GET WHAT YOU GET

by Julie Gassman   illustrated by Sarah Horne

Melvin did not deal well
with disappointment.

If his cookie had half as many chocolate chips as his sister's, **LOOK OUT!**

If he lost his turn during a game,
STAND BACK!

And if he didn't get exactly what he wanted . . .

well, you know . . .

"Sorry, Melvin, they were out of dinosaur backpacks."

No, Melvin did **NOT** deal well
with disappointment.

And this is why he **HATED**
his teacher's favorite rule.

Because of this rule, Melvin could not throw a
fit if he had to use crayons instead of markers.

He could not throw a fit if he ended up last in line.

He couldn't even throw a fit if his napkin
was pink instead of green.

"Oh, well," mumbled Melvin, "at least I can still
throw a fit at home. My family doesn't know
a thing about that TERRIBLE rule."

But that night when *it* was Melvin's turn to choose the movie, things changed. As soon as he'd chosen *Dinosaur Rumble*, his sister stomped her foot and whined,

"But I want to watch
A Pony Called Trouble!"

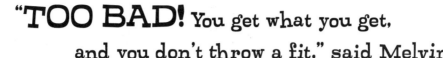

"**TOO BAD!** You get what you get, and you don't throw a fit," said Melvin.

Everyone stopped and looked at Melvin.

"What did you say?" asked Dad.

"You get what you get, and you
don't throw a fit," repeated Melvin.

"So if your cookie only has a few chocolate chips, you shouldn't throw a fit?" asked his sister.

"And if you lose a turn during a game,
you shouldn't throw a fit?" asked his dad.

"And if the dinosaur backpacks are all sold out, you should be happy with the robot one, and you absolutely should not throw a fit?" asked his mom.

Melvin gulped. There was no way to take it back.

EVERYONE KNEW.

"Well, I mean, at school you shouldn't throw a fit, 'cause that's the rule. But at home, you can," he said.

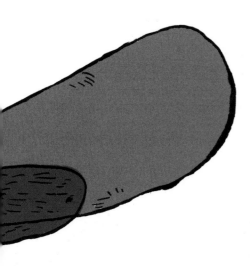

"I think that sounds like a good rule for at home, too," said Dad.

"I agree!" said Mom.

"Home and school, that's the rule!" his sister chanted.

Melvin wanted to **CRY.**

He wanted to **SHOUT.**

He wanted to lie down on the ground and **THROW** his arms and legs about.

But he didn't.

After all, you get what you get,
and you don't throw a fit.

To Tricia, Gina, and Paulette.
The original, and my favorite,
nonstop talkers! -CJ

For my amazing family and friends. -RW

Little ✦ BOOST is published by

Picture Window Books
A Capstone Imprint
1710 Roe Crest Drive
North Mankato, Minnesota 56003
www.capstonepub.com

Library of Congress Cataloging-in-Publication data is
available on the Library of Congress website.

ISBN: 978-1-5158-1882-3 (saddle-stitch)

Designer: Kay Fraser

Printed and bound in China.
005007

Lacey Walker, NONSTOP TALKER

BY CHRISTIANNE JONES
ILLUSTRATED BY RICHARD WATSON

PICTURE WINDOW BOOKS
a capstone imprint

Lacey Walker was quite the little talker.

She liked to **talk.**

And **talk.**

And **talk.**

"**Lacey,** please stop talking and eat your lunch," chided her mom.

"**Lacey**, less talking and more listening," scolded her teacher.

"**Lacey,** please quit talking! I can't hear my movie!" shouted her brother.

"**Lacey,** stop talking and brush your teeth," sighed her dad.

Nothing could quiet little Lacey.
She talked and talked and **talked**.

But on one gloomy Monday morning, all that talking caught up with her. Lacey Walker **lost her voice.**

She tried to whisper.

She tried to **SHOUT!**

She tried to **sing**.

But nothing happened.

Lacey **moped** through breakfast.

However, it didn't take her nearly as long
to eat since she **couldn't talk.**

Lacey even had time to finish her homework!

"I'm really on a roll this morning,"

she thought.

Lacey **moped** on her walk to school.

However, Lacey realized her friend Nadine told great jokes and was **really funny.**

"Odd that I never noticed that before," Lacey thought.

Lacey **moped** all day at school.

However, she finished all of her work and got a **gold star** for listening.

"I've never gotten a gold star before," she thought.

That night, Lacey wasn't quite so **mopey**.
She grabbed a snack and watched a monster
movie with her brother.

"He was right," she thought.
"This movie is awesome!"

And when her dad came upstairs, Lacey was ready for bed. Her teeth were brushed, her pajamas were on, and she was lying quietly in her bed.

They even had time to read **two extra books!**

The next morning, Lacey woke up feeling great!
Not only could she talk again, but she could whisper.
She could shout! She could sing.

"This is the best day EVER!"
Lacey declared.

Lacey raced downstairs, **talking** the entire way.

"Oh my goodness! I have so much
to say," Lacey said. "Nadine is hilarious!
Gold stars are the best! I like monster movies . . .

. . . but first, I'm going to eat my breakfast," Lacey said with a **smile.**

And as Lacey quietly ate her breakfast,
her family talked, and she **listened.**

Lacey Walker still liked to talk.

And **talk.**

And **talk.**

But she liked to listen once in a while, too.

For Steve.
"Shyness is nice,
but shyness can stop you."
— bb

Little Boost is published by
Picture Window Books
A Capstone Imprint
1710 Roe Crest Drive
North Mankato, Minnesota 56003
www.capstonepub.com

Library of Congress Cataloging-in-Publication Data
Bracken, Beth.
 Too shy for show-and-tell / by Beth Bracken ; illustrated by
Jennifer Bell.
    p. cm. – (Little boost)
Summary: Sam is so shy that nobody knows much about
him, but when he must stand in front of his class for show-
and-tell, he finds the courage to share.
 ISBN 978-1-5158-1879-3 (saddle-stitch)
[1. Bashfulness–Fiction. 2. Show-and-tell presentations–
Fiction. 3. Schools–Fiction.] I. Bell, Jennifer A., ill. II. Title.
III. Series.
 PZ7.B6989Too 2011
 [E]–dc22   2010050939

Creative Director: Heather Kindseth
Art Director: Kay Fraser
Designer: Emily Harris

Printed and bound in China.
005007

Too Shy for Show -and- Tell

by Beth Bracken

illustrated by Jennifer Bell

PICTURE WINDOW BOOKS
a capstone imprint

Sam was a quiet boy.

Nobody knew much about him.

Sam loved trucks, but nobody knew that.

Sam's favorite food was chocolate cake,
but nobody knew that.

Sam thought dogs were the best animals in the world,

but nobody knew that, either.

The only thing that people knew about Sam was that
he didn't talk much.

And Sam really didn't like talking in front of people,
which is why Sam hated show-and-tell.

Show-and-Tell Friday

On Wednesday, Miss Emily told the class that show-and-tell would be on Friday.

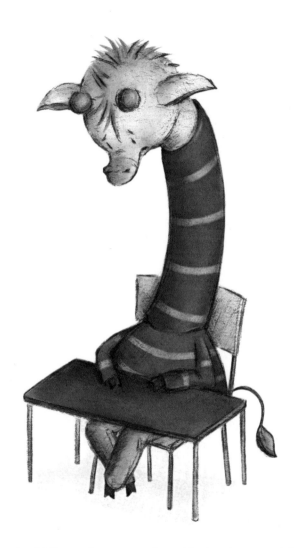

Sam spent most of Thursday worrying. He had a great thing to bring for show-and-tell, but he was scared.

On Friday, Sam didn't get out of bed.

"My tummy hurts," he lied.

"You're fine, and you need to go
to school today," his mom said.

At school, Sam told Miss Emily he'd forgotten
about show-and-tell.

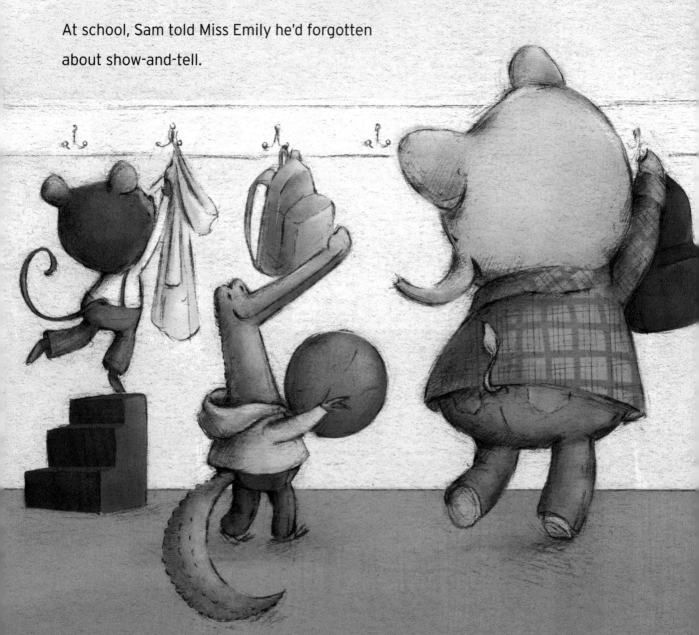

"I didn't bring anything," he said. But that wasn't true.

His perfect show-and-tell thing was in his backpack.

"That's okay," Miss Emily said. "You can just tell the class about the thing you forgot at home."

Sam was terrified. He didn't want to talk in front of everyone.

The thought of it made his tummy hurt really, really bad.

He imagined that he'd
say something dumb.

Or that he'd mess
up his words.

Or that he'd faint.

Or that he'd cry.

Sam watched the other kids show their show-and-tell things.

David showed some socks that his grandma had knitted him.

Everyone clapped when he was done.

Helena showed a new doll she got for her birthday.

Everyone clapped when she was done.

Otto showed a cool leaf that he found on the way to school.

Otto said "weaf" instead of "leaf," but nobody seemed
to notice, and everyone clapped when he was done.

Then it was Sam's turn. He got his perfect show-and-tell thing out of his backpack and went to the front of the room.

"What do you have to show us today, Sam?"

Miss Emily asked with a smile.

Sam took a deep breath. He looked out at his classmates.

They were quietly waiting.

Sam held up his picture. "This is my new dog," he said. "I named him Chocolate, because that's my favorite kind of cake, and he's the color of chocolate cake."

Sam didn't faint.

He didn't throw up.

He didn't cry.

And no one laughed.

Instead, everyone clapped
when he was done.

Now everyone in class knew
a little bit more about Sam.

Next time, he thought,
I'll bring my biggest truck.

And he did.

To Nathan, for putting up with me
when I am wearing my crabby pants. — jg

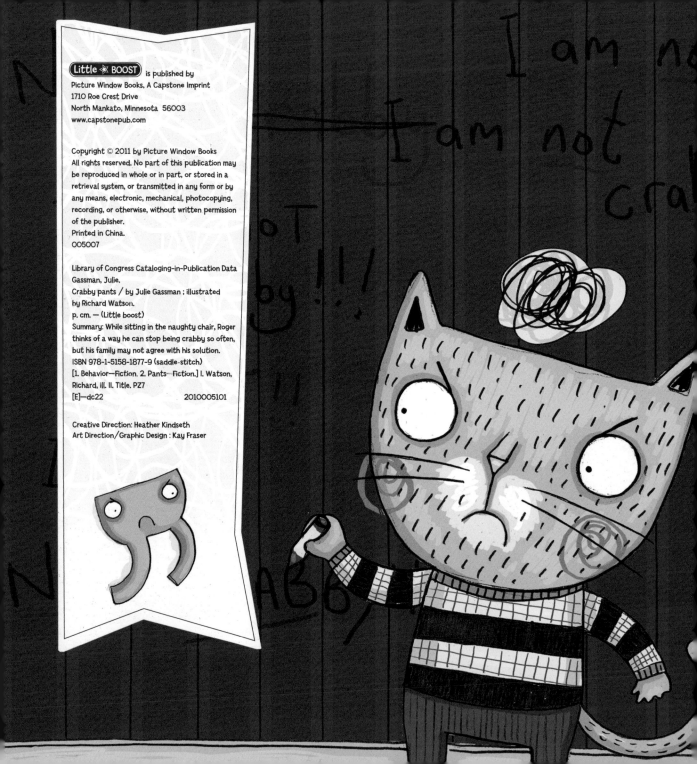

Little ★ BOOST is published by
Picture Window Books, A Capstone Imprint
1710 Roe Crest Drive
North Mankato, Minnesota 56003
www.capstonepub.com

Printed in China.
005007

Library of Congress Cataloging-in-Publication Data
Gassman, Julie.
Crabby pants / by Julie Gassman ; illustrated
by Richard Watson.
p. cm. — (Little boost)
Summary: While sitting in the naughty chair, Roger
thinks of a way he can stop being crabby so often,
but his family may not agree with his solution.
ISBN 978-1-5158-1877-9 (saddle-stitch)
[1. Behavior—Fiction. 2. Pants—Fiction.] I. Watson,
Richard, ill. II. Title. PZ7
[E]—dc22   2010005101

Creative Direction: Heather Kindseth
Art Direction/Graphic Design : Kay Fraser

Crabby

Pants

by Julie Gassman   illustrated by Richard Watson

PICTURE WINDOW BOOKS
a capstone imprint

This is Roger.

He gets CRABBY.

A lot.

There was the morning his older brother
ate the last frozen waffle.

Roger was stuck eating cereal.

Then there was the day Roger's class
was supposed to go to the zoo.

"We cannot go to the zoo in a thunderstorm,"
his teacher said.

And what about the day he fell asleep waiting for his favorite TV show to come on?

His mom let him sleep through the
whole thing!

There was only one thing to do...

get CRABBY.

"You shouldn't be such a crabby pants," his older brother said.

That made Roger even CRABBIER.

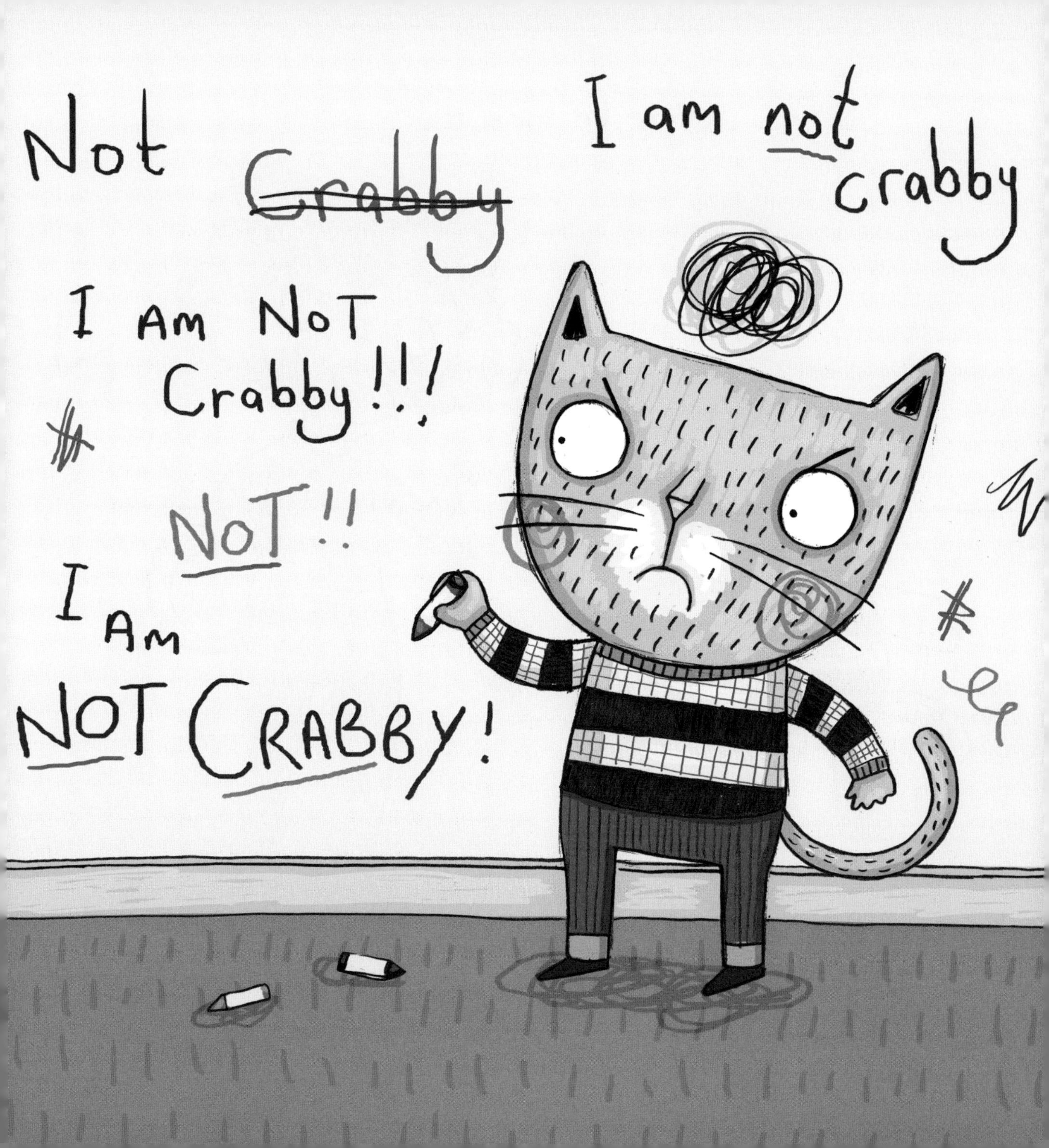

Not Crabby
I am not crabby
I AM NOT Crabby!!!
NOT!!
I AM NOT CRABBY!

Before he knew it,

Roger was sitting in the **naughty chair.**

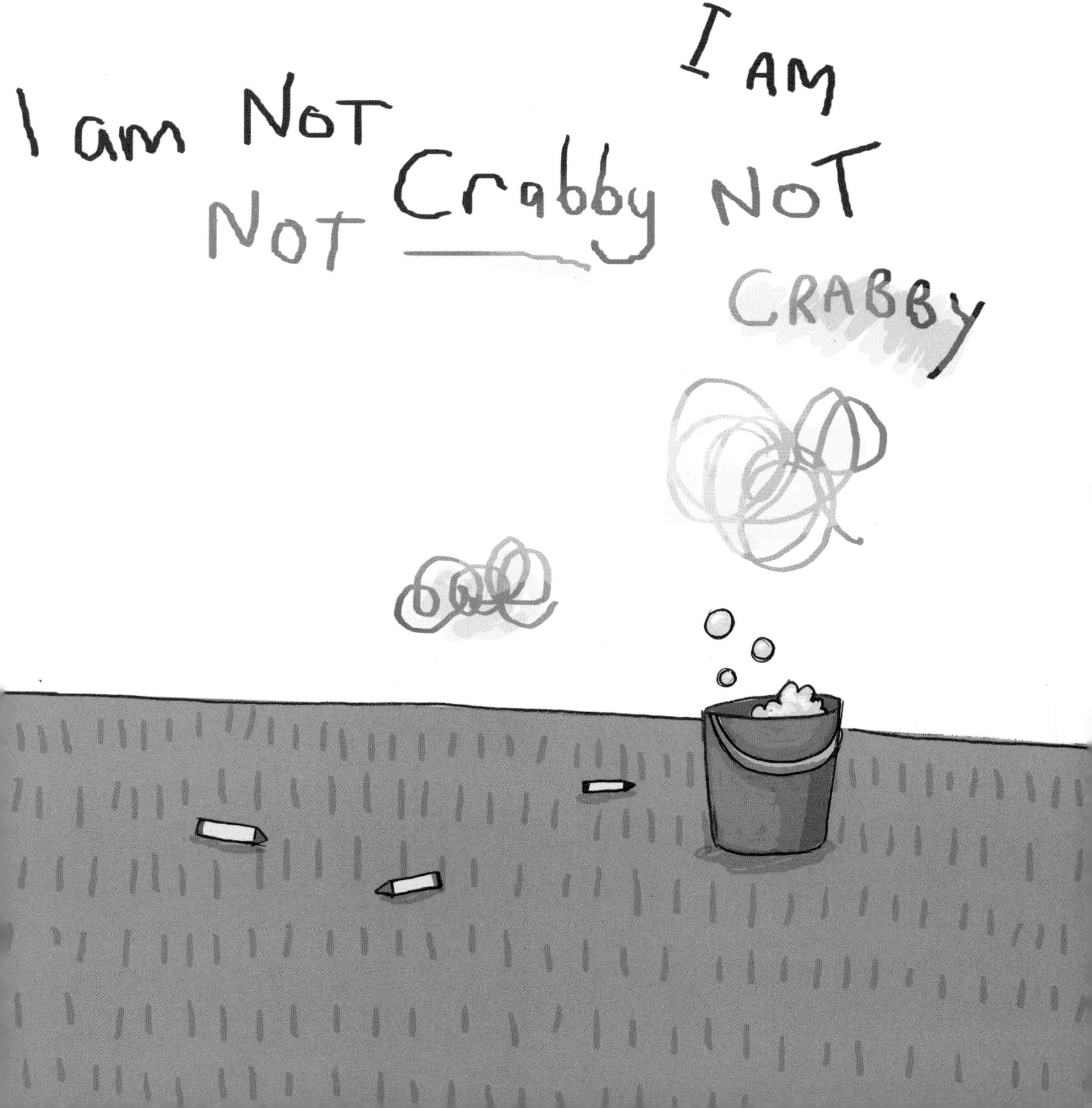
I am NOT
NOT
Crabby
I AM
NOT
CRABBY

Roger thought about what his brother had said.

Something CLICKED

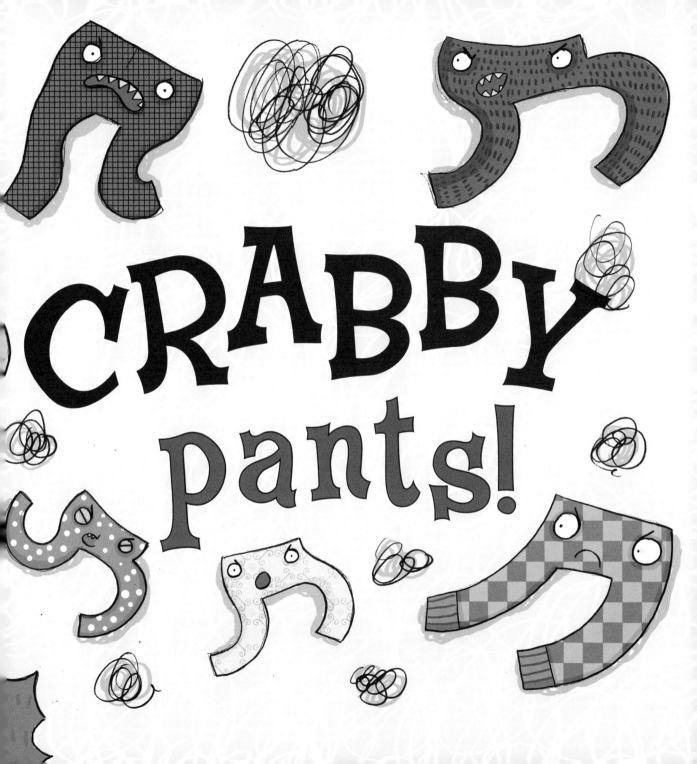

Roger thought of all the times he was crabby.
What did they all have in common?

His pants!

It was all clear now.

And Roger knew just what he had to do.

The next morning . . .

Roger showed his mom and dad how he had
solved his crabby problem.

"After all," said Roger,

"there's no such thing as

CRABBY

shorts."

Roger's mom and dad were not happy.

And soon, Roger was

CRABBY
again.

That night...

Roger decided to take care of the CRABBY pants problem once and for all.

The next morning, Roger's family discovered
what he had done.

"Isn't this great? Now, no one will ever get

CRABBY   again!" said Roger.

But he was
wrong.

For Ellen, Emily, and Julia.

Little Boost is published by
Picture Window Books
A Capstone Imprint
1710 Roe Crest Drive
North Mankato, Minnesota 56003
www.capstonepub.com

Library of Congress Cataloging-in-Publication Data
Bracken, Beth.
  The little bully / by Beth Bracken ; illustrated by Jennifer Bell.
    p. cm. -- (Little boost)
  Summary: When Fred makes fun of Billy at school, Billy has to
learn how to deal with his friend's bullying.
  ISBN 978-1-5158-1881-6 (saddle-stitch)
  1. Bullying--Juvenile fiction. 2. Schools--Juvenile fiction.
3. Friendship--Juvenile fiction. 4. Human behavior--Juvenile
fiction. [1. Bullies--Fiction. 2. Schools--Fiction. 3. Friendship-
-Fiction.] I. Bell, Jennifer A., ill. II. Title. III. Series: Little boost.
  PZ7.B6989Li 2012
  [E]--dc23
                           2011029540

Designer: Emily Harris

Printed and bound in China.
005007

The Little Bully

by Beth Bracken

illustrated by Jennifer A. Bell

PICTURE WINDOW BOOKS

a capstone imprint

Billy was a cool kid. He was nice to people. He was nice to animals. He had a nice smile, and he was very polite.

Billy had a lot of friends, and nobody was ever mean to him.

Well, nobody except **Fred**

Fred could see the tiniest stain on Billy's shirt.

"Billy spills EVERYTHING! What a slob!"

If Billy made one mistake when he was writing,
Fred would point and laugh.

"Billy can't even write his name!"

For show-and-tell, Billy brought a drawing of his family.

He thought it was pretty great.

But Fred couldn't stop laughing when he saw it.

"You used so much pink. That's a color for girls!"

Billy tried to stand up for himself. But no matter what he said,
Fred would just laugh.

It made Billy feel **horrible**.

Billy started to think
he wasn't **smart**.

Or **funny**.

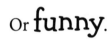

Or **nice** to look at.

Billy started to think that **nobody** liked him.

Billy didn't want to go to school anymore. But he didn't want to tell his mom or dad the real reason.

Instead, he said, "School is **dumb**. I just want to stay home."

"Going to school is your job," Dad told him.

"It's important for you to do your job," Mom said.

So Billy kept going to school, and Fred kept teasing him.

One day, Billy wore his favorite shirt to school. Of course, Fred made fun of it.

"You're wearing a baby shirt!"

Billy knew his shirt wasn't a baby shirt. He had a baby sister. Babies hardly even wore shirts. They usually wore pajamas, and they definitely didn't wear cool orange shirts with trucks on them.

Before Billy said anything, he looked at Fred.

Fred's shirt had a bear on it, he had paint on his pants,
and his shoes were untied.

Fred didn't have **any other friends** besides Billy, and it would be easy to make fun of him.

But Billy knew Fred's shoes were untied because it was hard to keep shoes tied.

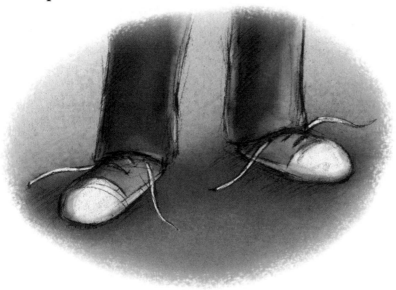

He liked Fred's bear shirt.

And they had been painting that morning, so **everyone** had paint on their pants.

So Billy tried something new.

"I like my shirt," he said bravely. "It's **not** a baby shirt."

"Well, your pants have paint all over them," Fred said.

"So do yours. And if you keep being mean to me, I won't play with you," Billy said.

Billy knew nobody else wanted to play with Fred.

Fred knew it, too.

After that, Fred wasn't mean to Billy. In fact, once he stopped
being mean, Fred became a really **cool** guy.

Just like Billy.